# Fickle Barbara

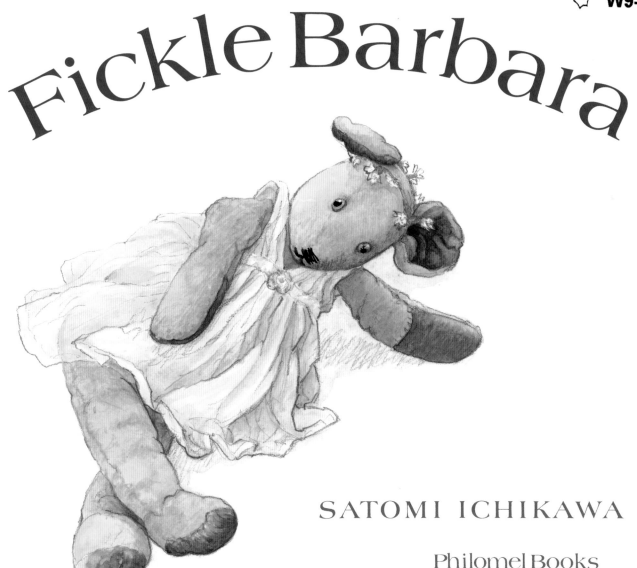

## SATOMI ICHIKAWA

Philomel Books

*For Ron and Pat*—S. I.

Ballerina Bear Barbara lived in a child's room in Paris with many many many other bears. But Barbara was allowed to stay on the child's bed as long as she wished.

Even so, Barbara did not like being alone for long. What she liked was her friend Ralph. Each day when the child left the room, she and Ralph would sit on the floor and chat and chat and chat. They were good old friends.

Then one day, Barbara decided she wanted new friends.
She met a handsome bear with a husky voice whose name was
Simon. They chatted, too, and sometimes sang.

She met a very funny bear whose name was Flora. She stood
on her head and made Barbara laugh.

She met Toby, a baby bear. "I love your smell of strawberry milk and vanilla biscuit!" she told him.

Bobo was the biggest bear she'd ever seen. And quite friend enough for Barbara!

Until she met Kiri the dancing bear, who could kick his heels as high as his head! Now there was a friend for Barbara.

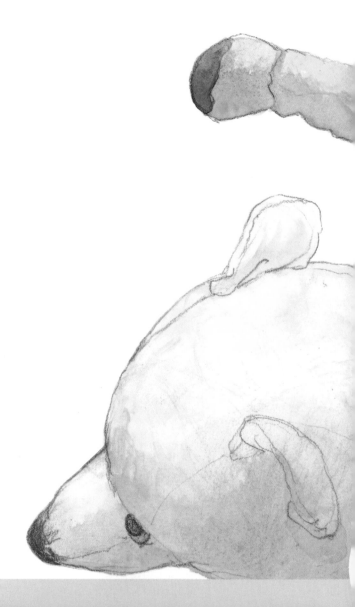

But Barbara found out the room was a big place: there were more bears to meet and know.

She met a bear with a medal, near the doorway

and artist bears in the toy box.

There is nothing like new friends, Ballerina Bear Barbara
said to herself. She had forgotten all about Ralph.

But then she met Zoe and Gatsby bear. When she asked them to play, they said no thank you, they had each other.

And when Barbara met Eddie, he greeted her with
a smile but said sorry, he couldn't play just now.

She met Grandmother bear, and asked her to play. She said she already had so many friends she didn't know what to do.

She met Angel bear, and asked her to play. Angel said she was sorry, thank you, that her cousins had arrived from the country and she needed to play with them.

A whole group of bears was sitting and laughing in a circle: Barbara loved circles and she loved to laugh. But the bears turned their back on Barbara and said, "No outsiders invited."

And some clowns were too busy
clowning to stop to play with Barbara.

Barbara sat down on the bedroom floor. She had gone a long
way from her place on the child's bed. She had met many new
friends: big bears and small ones, ones that stood on their head
and ones that wore medals. But what she missed was Ralph.

"But I'm still here, Barbara," a voice said. It was Ralph. The two sat down and chatted and chatted. Like old times.

"It is nice to find new friends, and I have a lot to tell you," Barbara said to him. "But it is nice to find old friends, as well."

And Ralph agreed with that.

Text by Patricia Lee Gauch

The artist used watercolor and pencil to create the illustrations for this book.

Copyright © 1993 by Satomi Ichikawa
Published by Philomel Books, a division of The Putnam & Grosset Group,
200 Madison Avenue, New York, NY 10016. All rights reserved.
This book, or parts thereof, may not be reproduced in any form without
permission in writing from the publisher. Published simultaneously in Canada.
Printed in Hong Kong by South China Printing Co., (1988) Ltd.
Book design by Gunta Alexander. The text is set in Goudy Old Style.
Library of Congress Cataloging-in-Publication Data
Ichikawa, Satomi. Fickle Barbara / Satomi Ichikawa.  p.  cm.
Summary: Ballerina Bear Barbara, who lives in a child's room in Paris, discovers
that while it is nice to make new friends, old friends should never be forgotten.
[1. Teddy bears—Fiction. 2. Friendship—Fiction.] I. Title.
PZ7.09715Ib  1993  [E]—dc20  92-23200  CIP  AC
ISBN 0-399-22020-8
1 3 5 7 9 10 8 6 4 2
First Impression